GHOST STORIES

JOHN TOWNSEND

SCRIBO

SCRIBO

First published in Great Britain by Scribo MMXVIII
Scribo, an imprint of
The Salariya Book Company
25 Marlborough Place, Brighton, BN1 1UB
www.salariya.com

ISBN 978-1-912233-52-6

The right of John Townsend to be identified as the author of this work has been
asserted in accordance with sections 77 and 78 of the Copyright, Designs
and Patents Act, 1988.

Book Design by Isobel Lundie

© The Salariya Book Company
MMXVIII

Text copyright © John Townsend

Printed and bound in China

www.salariya.com

Artwork Credits
Illustrations: Isobel Lundie

10

GHOSTLY TALES TO SEND A SHIVER THROUGH YOUR BONES...

7.   Introduction

9.   The Rabbit's Foot

23.   Cornerstone Cottage

37.   When the Clock Stops

53.   The Missing Finger

67.   The Skull

82.   The Last Train

94.   Behind You

108. The Midnight Passenger

118. The Mummy's Revenge

133. Something in the Cellar

144. Ghostly Facts

151. Glossary

GHOST STORIES

JOHN TOWNSEND

Stories that dabble in the unexplained, mysterious and 'just a bit creepy' have been told with relish in flickering firelight for thousands of years. Getting the shivers through storytelling (fear not, nothing too gruesome here) can even be said to help us confront some of our fears and develop the imagination for dealing with horrors of the real world. There's nothing quite like ghostly tales shared with others to unite mere mortals and quicken our collective pulses. After all, shivery stories have a long and rich tradition of nudging us from our comfort zones and tingling our twitchy nerves. Either that or they scare your pants off. Hold on tight!

THE RABBIT'S FOOT

According to ancient legend: 'The left hind foot of a rabbit caught at night in a cemetery has special powers.' A black rabbit's foot is not only very rare but also, according to folklore, has the power to grant three wishes. Carrying a rabbit's foot in a pocket as a lucky charm was quite common among country people many years ago. Even so, be careful what you wish for!

A cold wind rattled the windows and spattered the panes with tiny snowflakes. Mrs Wright peered out into the street, where the gas lamp spluttered its flickering light through a snowy flurry. Her husband shovelled more coal into the hearth and returned to his game of chess.

"I've got you this time, Dad," Eddie grinned. "It's checkmate!"

Before Mr Wright had time to check if his son had cheated, a loud knock on the front door clattered through the house. They all looked up, startled.

"Who can that be at this hour? I didn't see anyone approaching," Mrs Wright mumbled as she went to the door. An icy gust howled through the letterbox, swirling smoke down the chimney and across the room.

"I'll be surprised if we don't wake up to a blanket of snow in the morning," Eddie said. His father reached for a poker to liven up the flames.

"It's Mr Seers from number 28," his mother announced. "You'd best come in out of the cold.

The kettle has just boiled if you'd like a cup?"
she asked him.

"That's very kind, Mrs Wright. I don't mind
if I do. I hope I'm not disturbing your game of
chess, young Eddie – it's just that I felt the need
to come around for a little word. I trust you don't
mind this intrusion, Mr Wright."

Mr Seers was one of those neighbours who kept
himself to himself but was always happy to chat
at the gate or offer produce from his vegetable
garden in summer. Since losing his son in the
trenches at the start of the war, he and his ailing
wife were seldom seen in the town.

"Come and sit by the fire, Mr Seers – it will
soon perk up. We were just saying how the snow
looks set to settle. There again, you should know,
what with all your weather forecasting, country
folklore and your gift of seeing the future."

Removing his overcoat, Mr Seers sat by the
fire and stared into the smoke. "I'll come straight

to the point. It's my dream that I need to tell you about. As you know, some of my dreams have proved to warn of serious events. On those occasions, I was sadly unable to alter the course of history. I foresaw the tragedy of the *Titanic* before she sailed on that fateful voyage. I foresaw the outbreak of the Great War and its tragic events, long before the first bullet was fired. Thankfully, at last, that terrible conflict has ended but we have yet to learn the true human cost. But now, this time, after my dream the other night, there is time to act and avoid personal heartache for your family, Mr Wright."

Eddie pulled a face and headed to the door.

"I would prefer you stayed, young man," Mr Seers said, seriously. "My dream concerns you."

Eddie returned to sit beside the chessboard as the agitated neighbour shuffled awkwardly.

"How old are you now, Edward?" he asked, without looking up.

"Sixteen."

"And enjoying work at the mill?"

"It's all right. I'm learning how to fix some of the machines. It keeps me out of mischief."

His mother came in with a tray of teacups and set them on the table.

"I'll come straight to the point," Mr Seers repeated. "My dream warned of something unfortunate. Danger. It affects you, Edward – so I brought you this in the hope of warding off ill fortune." He fumbled in his pocket. "It's a lucky rabbit's foot. It's black and quite rare."

He rested it on the arm of his chair. "It's very old and has been well-used to good effect."

"A rabbit's foot?" said Mrs Wright, with total disgust.

"To look at," Mr Seers whispered, "it's just an ordinary little mummified left hind foot – but there's power in it, you mark my words."

"And what is there so special about it?" asked

Mr Wright suspiciously, as he picked up the rabbit's foot, examined it, then placed it gently on the table as the man in front of him answered very softly.

"It has the power to grant three wishes. I suggest you keep it... just in case. It might well save your son from harm. That's all I can say." He took one sip from his teacup, returned it to the tray and reached for his coat. "At least I have done what I could," he added, before looking directly at Eddie. "You can't say I didn't warn you, young man. Good luck."

As he left, a chilling draught entered the room, swirling more smoke from the chimney.

"That was all very creepy," Eddie laughed. "I think it's best if I throw this thing on the fire." He picked up the rabbit's foot and sneered, as his mother returned from seeing their visitor out.

"There's no harm in giving it a try, I suppose," his father said. "Pass it to me and I'll put it to the test."

"It's just silly nonsense," his wife snapped. "Anyway, whatever would you wish for?"

"A bit of cash might be nice," he giggled.

"How much do you need, Dad? How about a few million?" joked Eddie.

"That's just daft, love," Mrs Wright poured herself another cup of tea. "Mind you, I wouldn't mind a fresh set of fancy china plates and new curtains. A holiday would be nice. How about two hundred pounds?"

"More like five hundred," Eddie added. "Go on, Dad, give it a try."

His father gingerly gripped the rabbit's foot in his right hand, turned his back to the fireplace and said very slowly, "I wish for five hundred pounds."

A sudden whoosh of smoke and spray of sparks shot up the chimney, accompanied by his shuddering cry. His wife and son moved anxiously towards him.

"It moved," he cried, with a stare of horror at the rabbit's foot now discarded on the floor. "As I wished, it twisted in my hand like a snake."

"Well, I don't see any money," Eddie snorted, as he picked up the foot and placed it on the table, "and I bet I never shall."

His father, still stunned, shook his head. "Never mind, though; there's no harm done, but it gave me a shock all the same."

"Maybe you'll find the cash under your pillow," Eddie laughed when he went up to bed. "I'm on the early shift in the morning so I won't see you till tomorrow evening. Goodnight."

His mother went to bed shortly afterwards, leaving her husband sitting alone in the darkness, gazing at the dying fire. As he pondered, his hand grasped the rabbit's foot, and with a little shiver, he placed it on the mantelpiece and went up to bed.

GHOST STORIES

The snow was beginning to drift against walls and lampposts. By five o'clock in the evening, the sky had darkened and the streetlamps were lit. Mr Wright shovelled coal into the hearth as a loud knock on the front door clattered through the house. His wife looked up, startled.

"Who can that be? It's too early for Eddie to be home," she mumbled through the pins in her mouth while pinning a dress pattern to a length of fabric. "Go and see who it is, love."

Her husband returned with a young woman they didn't know. She wore a long, dark coat dusted with snow.

"I was asked to call," she announced, stooping to pick a piece of cotton from her shoe. "I've come from the mill."

Mrs Wright dropped the pins into her hand.

"Is something the matter?" she gasped. "Has anything happened to Eddie? What is it? What is it?"

Her husband tried to calm her. "There there, love – don't jump to conclusions. You've not brought bad news, I'm sure miss," he said, turning to the stranger.

"I'm sorry," she replied.

"Is he hurt?" his mother sobbed, as her husband held her hand.

"Badly hurt, I'm afraid," the woman answered quietly, "but he is not in any pain. Not now."

"Oh, that's a relief," his mother sighed, before realising what she'd meant.

"He was caught in the machinery," said the visitor. "I'm sorry. There was nothing anybody could do." After a long silence, she added, "The firm wishes me to convey their sincere sympathy for your great loss. Please understand, I am just obeying orders in conveying the sad news, but..."

she paused and shuffled awkwardly. "They admit no blame, but in consideration of your son's services, they wish to present you with a sum of money as compensation."

Mr Wright dropped his wife's hand and stared with horror. His dry lips shaped the words, "How much?"

"Five hundred pounds," came the chilling reply.

"Where can I see him? I want to see Eddie before he's laid to rest," his mother pleaded.

"That's up to you," the woman answered coldly, "but it may be best to remember him as he was. His face and body were badly disfigured and..."

"I think it would be best if you left us now," said Mr Wright sharply. He briskly ushered her to the door and returned to comfort his wife. After dabbing at her tears, she stood and whispered, "The foot. The rabbit's foot. I want it."

SHIVERS

"It's there – on the mantelshelf where I left it," he replied. "Why?"

"I only just thought of it," she cried. "Why didn't I think of it before? Why didn't you think of it?"

"Think of what?"

"The other two wishes," she grabbed the rabbit's foot and put it in her husband's hand before blurting, "We've only had one. We can wish Eddie alive again."

"You don't know what you are saying."

"WISH!" she cried.

"It's foolish and wicked."

"WISH!" she repeated.

He raised his hand. "I wish my son alive again."

The rabbit's foot fell to the floor, and they both sat in stunned silence, listening to the ticking of the clock. After almost a minute, a very gentle knock came from the front door, so quiet they hardly heard it. Neither of them moved until the knock was repeated, louder this time, followed by a third persistent tapping, this time at the window.

"WHAT'S THAT?" she cried. "It must be Eddie!" She ran to the door, but her husband was close behind, catching her by the arm and holding her tightly.

"What are you going to do?" he shouted.

"It's my boy, it's Eddie!" she panted. "What are you holding me for? Let go. Open the door."

"No! Don't let it in," he yelled.

"You're afraid of your own son," she snapped. "Let me go. I'm coming, Eddie."

There was another knock, and then another. She rattled back the chain and pulled at the bolt. By now the knocking was frantic and the door shook violently.

"The bolt," she gasped. "I can't reach it."

Her husband was on his hands and knees,

groping madly on the floor for the rabbit's foot. If only he could find it before the thing outside got in. The front door shuddered from the thumping and clawing at the outside.

Just as his wife stretched up and clattered back the bolt, Mr Wright grasped the rabbit's foot and frantically breathed his third and final wish. The knocking suddenly stopped, but the echoes continued through the house. They were drowned by a cold wind rushing and howling through the letterbox, and a long loud wail from his wife as she pulled open the front door and screamed into the night.

The street lamp flickering opposite shone on a quiet and deserted road. Ghostly footprints in the snow leading to the front door were already disappearing as another flurry swept in on a bitter, silent wind.

CORNERSTONE COTTAGE

I've never gone back to the tiny village just a mile from the sea. As children, we spent great summers there; chasing through the wheat fields, exploring the woods or picnicking on vast sandy beaches before plunging into the waves. Only once did we stay at Cornerstone Cottage. Once was enough.

With just two bedrooms upstairs and a small

box room on the ground floor beyond the kitchen (where I slept), the cottage was just big enough for four of us. There was only one main room downstairs, with a front door opening from it onto a country lane filled with tractors chugging along. Outside, the walls were old redbrick and flint, just like the other cottages all joined in a row. Hundreds of years ago they were all part of one big farmhouse, with Cornerstone Cottage on the end, having once been part of the old dairy. The yard next to it still had chickens clucking from early morning, and the whole place seemed to be locked in a world from long ago. There was electricity but no gas, phone, Wi-Fi signal or any other connections to the real world. The owners who rented it to holidaymakers proudly advertised it as a place to 'switch off from the rat race'. But they didn't mention everything. Some of Cornerstone Cottage's secrets remained for us to discover for ourselves.

GHOST STORIES

The first time I sensed something mysterious was an evening after a blisteringly hot day on the beach. We'd been invited to a barbecue but, as I'd left my T-shirt back at Cornerstone Cottage, I walked back across the fields to collect it. Being eleven, I was happy to go by myself but as soon as I put the key in the door, I heard a scuttling sound from inside. I called out "Is anyone there?" as I went in. No reply. When I got to my bedroom, I was sure I'd left my T-shirt flung on the bed but it was folded neatly on a chair. It was then I heard the noise upstairs – like a heavy object being dragged across the floor. I slowly climbed the stairs, expecting to find the owners had come to rearrange the furniture – but there was no one. Nothing had moved and there was nothing unusual. The only thing that freaked me out was a line of dolls on a shelf on the landing. They were Victorian dolls in fancy costumes, with porcelain faces and big gawping eyes – and I was convinced they were all staring at me. I darted back downstairs, grabbed my stuff and ran from the cottage.

Although my sister and parents agreed with me about the creepy dolls on the landing, they just humoured me about the noises upstairs. "That's old houses for you," my dad said, "they creak and groan as the wooden floors shrink or expand. In this heat, the old timbers in the roof will be stretching a bit so there'll be all kinds of noises, I expect."

That put my mind at rest, even though I wasn't totally convinced. I didn't think any more about it until we got back to the cottage after dark. I sat down to watch the TV, even though the reception was hopeless and the picture went all wobbly. As I switched it off, my mother came downstairs and gave me one of her 'you annoying little pest' looks.

"What have I done now?" I asked.

"How many times must I tell you to tidy up after yourself? I've just spent the last five minutes putting everything back in the airing cupboard. There wasn't any need to throw out the towels across the floor, you know."

"I haven't been anywhere near the airing cupboard," I insisted.

"Durrr – you came back for your T-shirt, remember? That's where I saw it last," my sister chipped in to make me look stupid. I told them exactly where my T-shirt had been, but I was beginning to doubt myself. Had I looked for it in the airing cupboard? But then I knew something weird was happening when Mum told me off again. "I know none of us likes those dolls on the landing, but there's no need to turn them all round to face the wall."

However much I insisted I hadn't touched the 'freaky things', everyone just looked at me with 'we don't believe you' on their faces. I got that a lot. I reckon the youngest in the family must get used to being disbelieved – it goes with the job. Sure, I was always winding them up – but I wasn't a serial liar. "You've got to believe me!" I shouted, only to be told we were all getting tired and needed to go to bed.

As soon as I switched off the light and put my head on the pillow, I heard the slightest high-pitch whine coming from a wardrobe in the corner. However many times I switched on the light, opened the wardrobe, searched inside and rearranged everything on the shelves, as soon as I got back to bed the sound started again. Of course, when I asked the others if they could hear it, they denied it.

"You and your imagination," my sister said.

"It's a well-known fact that old fogies can't hear high-pitched sounds like eleven-year-olds can," I retorted.

"I expect it's a little mosquito," Mum said.

"Put on some insect repellent and you'll be fine."

But I wasn't fine. Every time I woke in the night, I heard that annoying whine. Sometimes it woke me up when it got much louder. By breakfast time, I was extra grumpy.

"I hate my room," I sulked.

"At least you saw the error of your ways and turned the dolls back again," my sister said between mouthfuls of cereal.

"I haven't touched them!" I snapped.

"No, dear – I did," Mum smiled.

Just then there was a knock on the door and she went to answer it. A woman stood on the step, holding out some money.

"I've just come to pay you for the eggs," she said.

"You must have the wrong house," my mother answered.

"No, it was definitely this one – Cornerstone Cottage. The lady yesterday afternoon kindly sold me half a dozen eggs but as she didn't have any change, she told me to come back with the money this morning."

"What lady?"

"I assumed she was the farmer's wife. Big apron, quite old-fashioned looking. Quietly spoken. She took the eggs from that dresser right there inside the door. Lovely eggs – we just had a couple for breakfast." She pushed the money into my mother's hand and went, leaving us all staring at one another.

"There's bound to be a logical explanation," my father said. "I expect the owners of this place sometimes sell eggs at the door. Maybe Mrs Leggett dropped by yesterday and let herself in with her key."

I could tell even Dad didn't believe his own words. We all knew the owners had gone abroad for two weeks. The man next door had already told us the hens had stopped laying and there weren't any eggs for sale.

When we came back from the beach in the evening, I dreaded to think what we might find at the cottage. I had a good look around to see if anything was out of place but everything was just as we'd left it. That was a relief – so I went to bed reassured and very tired.

I was woken in the night by the whining sound again – but that wasn't all. The floor in my room was creaking, as if someone was walking past my bed. Or was it the sound of a rocking chair, slowly swaying to and fro on the wooden floor? I opened my eyes and stared into the darkness but couldn't see a thing. Suddenly I felt a jolt, like a bump at the end of the bed. I held my breath and listened. The whining stopped but it felt just as if someone was sitting on the corner of my bed... and knitting! I was convinced I heard the clicking of knitting needles.

I fumbled to switch on the bedside lamp and

when the light glared in my face, I turned to stare at the end of the bed. Nothing. I was in a sweat and my heart was racing but everything was perfectly normal. I told myself to get a grip and go back to sleep. I left the light on, just in case. It took me ages to fall asleep and I was woken by the birds at six o'clock in the morning. Sunlight was already streaming into my room and I sighed with relief. I glanced at the end of my bed and froze. There was a dent in the duvet where someone had been sitting. I scrambled out of bed in a panic, the duvet slipping onto the floor and destroying all evidence of the dent.

Everyone else was still asleep so I watched some random TV programmes but that horrible high-pitched whining seemed to be coming from the television now. I quickly switched it off and went upstairs to the bathroom. The sound seemed to follow me up there, too. As I had an itchy row of insect bites in the shape of a letter

C on my neck, I looked in the cabinet for some cream to rub on them. It was empty so I dabbed on cold water from the tap but I couldn't turn it off again. The water wouldn't stop flowing – constantly trickling and spluttering, however tightly I turned it. Now I'd get the blame for something else.

At breakfast, I explained about the noises and how someone had sat on my bed in the night. Of course, no one believed me and I was told again about my vivid imagination. My dad said I was clumsy, too, and he'd have to phone for a plumber as he couldn't fix the tap, either. I wasn't ready for the next accusation when my mother went to get some eggs from the old Welsh dresser.

"When did you do this?" She held up an open box of eggs. Each of the six eggs inside had been smashed. "These were perfectly alright yesterday when I checked them," she said. "You must try to be more careful."

SHIVERS

I stomped from the room in a strop. I was getting fed up with being blamed for everything, and I was surer than ever that something creepy was going on, even though no one else believed me. My dad was cross because he had to drive miles to get a phone signal and arrange for a plumber to call that morning while we were crabbing on the pier. We left a key under the wheelie bin at the side of the cottage and that was all there was to it – or so we thought.

When we arrived back at Cornerstone Cottage, the front door was wide open. My father called, "Hello, is anyone there?" Silence. We all slowly crept upstairs. On the landing, the airing cupboard was wide open and all the towels were thrown everywhere. Each of the dolls lay in the bath, all their heads removed. The tap was still running.

When my father came back from phoning the plumber, he sat down completely stunned.

"The plumber said that as soon as he arrived here and took out his tool box, his spanner and screwdriver moved across the floor on their own. He said he was hit on the head by a raw egg and heard a woman laugh. He grabbed his stuff and ran from the cottage."

A few weeks later, when we'd finally stopped talking about the strange goings-on at Cornerstone Cottage, my mum got a phone call. It was the owners of the cottage, who'd just got back from their holiday abroad.

"Was everything all right?" Mr Leggett asked. There was a long silence after Mum told him.

"Ah, I see," came the reply at last. "Not everyone meets her – just those she likes, it seems. We didn't warn you as you can never tell if she'll appear. You see, you shared Cornerstone Cottage with Mrs Coombs. She can be quite unpredictable but at least you survived a full week. Some don't. Apparently, she was the dairy maid long ago... before she passed away while knitting in her rocking chair in the back room. All very mysterious. They say she was found with a row of insect bites in the shape of a letter C on her neck."

WHEN THE CLOCK STOPS

When they wander from the expedition party, fifteen–year–olds Liam and Sacha are alone on the moors. Lost. At first, it's no big deal, as the map shows a hostel isn't too far away. But they haven't bargained on what is waiting in the darkness, and on what will happen on the night the clocks go back...

Liam threw down his rucksack and pulled

off his hiking boots. He fell onto the grass with a groan. "I never want to go on a hike again. Never. They said the Bronze Award expedition would be a piece of cake. I'm dying for a piece of cake right now. My feet are killing me. I give up – where are we?"

Sacha gulped from her water bottle. She sank to her knees, sitting on her mud-caked boots. "I haven't got a clue. Right now, I don't care."

Liam bit into a mini Mars Bar then handed her the rest. "Make the most of this last bite. No more left after this."

Sacha passed him the bottle. "Just a few sips. There's hardly any left."

Clouds cast deepening shadows over the hills. A large bird of prey rose in the sky and soared above the moor.

"This map doesn't make sense. I'm sure we turned left at the church in the village." Liam traced his finger over the map. "It doesn't agree with my phone, either. The GPS is useless. The signal's no good out here in the middle of nowhere. It keeps cutting out."

"My battery's virtually given up the ghost. Just like me," Sacha sighed before adding wearily, "I think we should go back. We know there's a pub a few miles back. I'd kill for a plate of hot chips." She looked up. "There's a huge bird up there. It must be a vulture waiting for us to die of thirst."

Liam turned the map round. "Unless that clump of trees is this bit of green on the map and on my phone." He swore when he lost the signal again.

Sacha laughed. "Let's face it, you haven't got a clue."

He kept looking at the map. "There's a red triangle thing marked here. It's a youth hostel. We can't be far off. Let's go there. Hostels are cheap. It's only a couple of miles."

Sacha got to her feet. "If you say so. It'll be

dark soon." She stared up at the circling bird with a growing sense of doom, as Liam put on his rucksack with a renewed burst of enthusiasm. "We'll be in the dry before the rain starts."

They linked arms and began walking towards the setting sun – towards the bird of prey and the dead of night.

The first drops of rain began to fall as Sacha pulled on the hood of her raincoat.

"How much further, Liam? My blisters say it's bed time."

"Not far. I'll be able to tell when we get to the top of this hill. We'll see down into the next valley. I should get a better phone signal up there."

Sacha snorted. "It'll be dark by the time we get to the top."

Thunder clouds blotted out the rising moon and rolled across the moor as a shriek filled the darkening sky. Liam and Sacha stopped to look up. A black shape swooped over their heads.

"Scary!" Sacha frowned. "That bird is like an omen. An angel of doom!"

Their boots squelched through mud. "Not long," Liam called. "We'll soon be at the top."

A flash of lightning snaked across the sky and a loud crack rumbled over the moor. "It's like something from a horror movie," Sacha panted. The rain swept across in silvery squalls. At the top of the hill Liam pointed into the next valley. "That must be the hostel. Down there. With the tall chimney and smoke."

"I don't like the look of it," Sacha murmured.

"It won't take us long," Liam said, ignoring her. The air was now very still. As they walked down towards the hostel, a strange silence fell. There was no rain here and everything was deathly still – apart from a bird hovering above the smoke that rose towards the pale moon peeping through parting clouds.

SHIVERS

A sign by a set of black iron gates said 'Youth Hostel. Members Only'. Just beyond stood a stark Gothic mansion surrounded by bent and twisted tree trunks.

Apart from a faint glow from one of the large upstairs windows, the house was in eerie darkness.

"I told you we'd find it," Liam said, smiling.

Sacha wasn't so sure. "It doesn't look very nice," she said.

Liam ignored her and added, "I've got cash. They'll let us stay the night."

Clanging through the gate, they walked along the path, up some crumbling steps and to the porch. A pair of boots caked in dried mud lay on the top step. Liam slammed his fist on the heavy door and a hollow thud echoed before the door swung open. A dimly lit hallway with dark oak panels stretched in front of them. The smell of soot drifted out over the porch. A thin, bent man in black stood in front of them. He had a hooked nose and small beady eyes. "Yes? What is it?" he croaked. His eyes stared like a bird's.

"Can we stay the night?" Liam said. "I can pay with a card or cash."

The man blinked. The light from a single bulb cast his shadow over the front steps. He had a shadow like a vulture's.

"Members only," he said. "You'll have to join."

"How much?"

"We've got rules," the man continued, not listening. "No matches. No paraffin. No time."

Sacha squeezed Liam's hand. She could smell drink on the man's breath.

"Are you the warden?" Liam asked.

The man ignored him. "It's late. It's only because of the clocks I can bend the rules tonight. We're full. One of you will have to sleep in the attic. The other in the boiler room."

Sacha pulled a face. "I don't like the sound of

that."

"Take it or leave it," he said with a hunch of his shoulders.

He moved his head in short, sharp jabs, like a crow.

"Any chance of some hot food?" Liam asked.

The man spoke but his eyes seemed far away. "Too late. Everyone's in bed. No flames." He stood back to let them in. A grand wooden staircase was lit by a fizzing gas lamp that spluttered, making the long shadows in the room shiver.

"You pay now. It'll be fifteen each," the warden squawked.

"Fine," Liam said, passing him two twenty-pound notes.

The warden clawed at them with his bony, talon-like fingers. "Is this a joke? You'll have to get your change in the morning. You'll have to do a duty. It's to get the milk from the farm at six o'clock. The farm is a mile up the track by the old stables. Sign this register."

Liam wrote his name in a dusty old book on a desk. He looked around for a computer screen, assuming he'd need to register on their system.

"Is there free Wi-Fi? I need to contact my dad." He caught sight of the last entry in the book. "The last person in this book got the date wrong. Wrong year!"

The man ignored him and gazed out from the door into the night.

"I'm dying to charge my phone and have a nice hot shower," Sacha smiled. "That's extra," the warden rasped. "Another five." He wrote on a pad and shuffled sheets of paper as Sacha reached into her pocket. "No problem. I've got a fiver. There you are."

For the first time, the man looked up into her eyes. His beady stare gave her the creeps. His eyes fixed on her like a hawk. "What's this?" he sneered. "That's not real money. Anyway, it's not five pounds. I want five shillings."

A grandfather clock chimed under the stairs. They counted each strike. Eleven. The man gave a sigh. "One more hour. I must do the clock before..." He stared blankly.

"Are you all right?" Sacha asked.

"Get to your rooms. One hour... till the clocks."

He fluttered off with a flapping of papers... like wings.

"Back to his perch!" Sacha whispered, stifling a giggle.

Liam smiled. "At least we've got a roof over our heads. I'll help you find the attic. It's all very quiet."

"Apart from that clock. It's weird. He said this place is full tonight. Where is everyone?"

The floorboards creaked as Liam and Sacha walked up the staircase. All the doors were shut on the first landing. A wooden spiral stairway led up to the attic, a tiny room with a bunk in the corner. Moonlight seeped in through a dusty skylight.

"Mmm. Nice," Sacha smirked. "You can treat me to a smart hotel tomorrow. We'll have a ten-course meal, too. So much for my plate of chips tonight. I can't believe it's so late. You'd better go to the boiler room. Sleep well. Don't get too hot!"

Liam looked at his watch. "I think my watch has stopped."

It was as Liam turned to leave that an orange flash filled the night and bloodcurdling screams ripped through the entire house.

The attic door flew open as a spray of sparks swept in. A sheet of flames tore up to the ceiling with a roar. Liam slammed the door, staring in horror at smoke pouring in underneath.

"There's no way out," Sacha screamed. "The stairs are on fire."

Smoke rose up through the red-hot floorboards

as Liam yelled, "Quick – push the bunk by the skylight. We'll have to climb up on the roof. Grab as many blankets as you can."

Churning smoke filled the attic. In a mad panic, with no idea what was beyond the window, they clambered out through the skylight onto the roof. Suddenly the room below them burst into a swirl of flames. Sparks flew up through the shattered window as thick black smoke rolled around them.

Sacha clawed her way to the edge of the roof where a drainpipe ran down the corner of the building. "Tie the blankets into a rope," she cried.

A jet of flame shot through the roof, creating a clatter of broken tiles. Liam frantically tied the end blanket around the pipe and Sacha climbed out over the gutter. The heat scorched their faces as they scrambled down through choking smoke. The whole house was a furnace by the time they landed with a thud on the ground, with more screams filling the night.

Liam shouted, "There's no way we can get back in to save anyone. The nearest house is the farm down there somewhere. We have to raise the alarm."

He grabbed Sacha's arm and they ran. Flames leapt into the sky behind them. They glanced back to see the sky glowing orange through the trees.

Gasping for breath, Liam and Sacha ran on through the night. At last they saw a light from a house ahead of them. Liam ran up the steps and thumped on the door. "Help! Quick! Fire! It's the youth hostel. Hurry!"

A man came to the door in seconds.

"Please help us," Sacha screamed. "It's terrible back there."

"Come in," he said calmly. "We thought you might come."

Sacha screamed again, "Don't you understand?

We must get help. Phone 999."

"It's OK. We understand." A woman appeared in the hallway. She, too, was very calm. "Don't worry any more. Come in and have a nice cup of tea."

The farmer led Liam and Sacha into the sitting room.

"There's no fire," he said slowly. "This happens every year."

His wife added, "It's the night the clocks go back. We'll tell you the story. We always stay up tonight. Just in case. We usually get someone up here."

The farmer looked at his watch. "You've done well. They usually take longer than this."

Sacha held on to Liam. Her hands were still shaking.

"But the youth hostel is burning down!" Liam shouted. "This isn't a joke."

"No, dear. It isn't a joke. The place burnt down

years ago. Before you were born." The farmer's wife smiled. "We remember it well. It was soon after we moved here. We were just putting all the clocks back when a young couple came knocking at the door. They were just like you. It was terrible. Over sixty people were killed that night. The warden used to keep cans of paraffin in the boiler room. They think he went in to change the time-switch and fell. He was fond of his drink. The boiler room exploded. Fire ripped through all that wood in seconds. In the morning there wasn't much of the place left. Just the ruins. That's all there is today. There was talk of rebuilding it once but it's really not worth it."

Sacha shook her head. "But we saw it. The big house with the tall chimney."

"That's right," the farmer went on. "The minute the clocks go back. Each year is the same. There are beds ready for you here."

Liam looked at the kind old couple. He didn't

understand. He looked at Sacha and held her hand. He looked at his watch. It had stopped at midnight. The minute the clocks went back.

An autumn mist hung in the cold morning air. It was early when Liam and Sacha walked down the track. They had to take a look. They had to see the truth for themselves.

As they reached a bend, they climbed the bank and stared. The hostel wasn't there – just a blackened crumbling wall covered in ivy. Brambles grew from a pile of charred bricks. The remains of a chimney stretched up from the ruins – black against the misty morning sky. Looking down at them from a twisted pillar hunched a large bird of prey. Staring with piercing eyes. Like fire.

THE MISSING FINGER

The house isn't there now. Only stories remain... stories of ghostly shapes drifting through the trees. The house wasn't far from the church, which still stands proudly. New houses with neat lawns now hide the horrors of the past. No one would know anything had happened. Not unless they watch... and wait.

Janya knew about the stories. She'd seen

them in a book on ghosts in the school library, showing black and white pictures of the house. It looked creepy... eerie... scary – which was why she wanted to find out more. A visit to the village and a look around the church could give her some material for her talk on the new school radio station.

It was a hot August afternoon when Janya set off across the fields. She left the footpath and walked along the disused railway line. It was cooler here in the shade. She paused to take a swig from her water bottle and checked her phone. This was the life, she thought. She felt like a real reporter in search of the truth.

From the top of a hill, Janya could see for miles across open fields. It was then she saw the church tower ahead. It stood against a bank of dark cloud, with a buzzard wheeling above it. Janya's tablet reminded her of the story:

In 1863, Henry Bull built a big house for his

wife and 14 children. He was the vicar of Gorley. He didn't know his new house was built where a convent once stood. The old story told of a nun who was bricked up in the cellar and left to die. Her crime was falling in love with a monk and planning to run away with him, but they were caught. He was burned at the stake for his sins. Ever since, people say they have seen strange things: shapes in the moonlight, moving shadows across the grass, a nun sobbing in the trees. Stories tell of a cloaked man searching in the fog, the smell of smoke and a woman's hand clawing at the church door – a left hand with a gold ring set with a ruby on the forefinger. But that's not all... the engagement finger is missing. Before she was bricked up, her fourth finger wearing the monk's 'promise ring' had been cut off.

Janya walked through the graveyard as she thought about the terrible story. She peered into the porch of the church. It was cooler here.

Perhaps there would be something inside to tell her about the old house from long ago? There might even be something about the story of the nun and the monk. She turned the heavy door handle with a clunk but the door refused to budge. She'd just have to look around the outside instead and record the scene.

It was as Janya turned from the door that she saw the woman. Her dark shape was framed in the bright sunlight spilling into the porch.

"I hope I didn't scare you," the woman said.

"Just a bit," Janya answered with a nervous giggle.

"I've been watching you, dear." The woman pulled a chain of large iron keys from her cape.

"Watching me?"

"Oh yes, dear. I'm always watching." She pointed upwards to where a CCTV camera looked down at Janya. "We have to keep a look-out here, you know. After all, you can't be too careful these days, can you?"

Janya couldn't see the woman's eyes as her face was in shadow. A blue hood covered her hair. She seemed to read Janya's mind. "It looks like rain," she said. "I always dress for the worst. We could be in for a storm. Do you want me to let you inside?"

"Yes please. If it isn't any trouble."

"No trouble. I've come to do the flowers. They don't do themselves."

She brushed past Janya and rattled a key in the lock. The heavy door creaked open and she led the way into the church. It felt damp and cool inside. Janya shivered as she looked around, before reading plaques on the walls. There was no mention of Henry Bull or the nun. Nothing.

The woman was busy arranging flowers on a pedestal. Janya held up her phone. "Do you mind if I take a few pictures?" she asked.

"Do what you must, dear."

SHIVERS

Janya pointed her phone at the altar and then at a stained-glass window. A heavy curtain hung across the entrance to the tower. Janya pulled it back to see what was behind. It smelt musty.

A sudden noise behind her made Janya turn. It sounded like a man's scream. Staring down the aisle, she looked to where the woman had been arranging flowers. There was no one there. Nor were there any flowers. The space was empty. Janya was alone in the church.

The wind howled in the porch and rattled the door. The steady clunking of the clock echoed from the tower. Janya shivered and reached out to a pile of old books. A scrap of newspaper poked from one of them. The headline read "GORLEY – THE MOST HAUNTED VILLAGE."

It was from a few weeks ago and told of people who once lived in the old house by the church. They'd reported strange things. In the 1900s, residents heard whispers in bedrooms at night and footsteps on the stairs. Two maids saw a nun appear in the garden. Then there was the story of a woman who lived in the house in the 1930s. One night something hit her face. She was thrown out of bed. Her name appeared in shaky writing on the walls. Then a message warned the house would burn down. People came from far and wide to stare at the house. It was called the most haunted house in the country.

In 1939, the house caught fire in the middle of the night. By morning it was just a ruin. And that was how it stayed for years. The bulldozers eventually came and new houses were built on the land.

Janya looked at the photo of the old house. She'd seen it and read those stories before. But the next part was new. The latest part of the story happened only a few weeks ago. The owner of one of the new houses was having a new garage built. The builders dug down and found bricks. It was an old cellar. Its doorway had been bricked-up. Inside they found a skeleton.

A photo in the paper showed a local 'ghost-hunter' pointing at the skull. But that wasn't all. Experts had done tests. They found the skeleton was of a woman who had lived hundreds of years ago. A bone on her left hand had been cut and the finger was missing. On another bony finger was a ring – with a ruby. Stamped in the gold was the sign of an old order of nuns.

Janya was desperate to get outside into bright sunshine. She reached out to turn the door handle but it wouldn't move. She was locked inside.

What was going on? First there was the strange woman who'd vanished and now the door had locked on its own. Suddenly, she felt an icy shiver. It was freezing by the door. How would she get out? She felt trapped... like the poor nun bricked up in her cellar.

The wind howled outside. A crack of thunder

echoed around the church. The door clattered as an icy blast ripped under it. Janya pulled and tugged at the handle. It just wouldn't move. "Help! Please let me out!" she cried.

The sickly smell of flowers stuck in her throat. But there were no flowers to be seen.

Janya tried to phone for help but the signal was dead. She rummaged through her bag and touched her water bottle. The water inside had turned to ice.

Hammering on the door, Janya cried. "Help me!" Her heart was pounding and her face was drenched in cold sweat. She coughed as the smell choked her. But it wasn't the smell of flowers this time. It was something else. Stronger. Deadlier. Smoke!

The loud crackle of flames filled the darkness behind her. "Help! Let me out!" she screamed.

From behind her she heard the rattle of curtain rings. She looked over her shoulder. The curtain was moving very slowly. It was being pulled back... by a pale, bony hand...

As she screamed, Janya clawed at the door. She kicked at it and drummed her fists on the solid oak. It was then that the latch lifted slowly. The door moved and swung open in a warm blast of air. Bright sunshine lit her face as a man stood in the doorway.

"Whatever's the matter with you, young lady?"

She threw herself at him. "You've got to help me. There's a fire... the woman... a hand..."

The man's face changed. "Utter nonsense," he snapped. "You kids are all the same. Snap out of it. There's nothing – look. It's all in the mind. You kids just like to make a fuss and get hysterical. Attention-seeking. A fuss over nothing."

The man was in a long black gown. He led Janya back into the church.

"Look. Nothing. Not worth all that screaming. Some children read all that ghost nonsense and believe it. I tell you, it's all made up. People should know better. I've been the verger here for years and I've never seen a ghost. It's utter rubbish."

"Verger?" Janya said. She was stunned. Almost in a trance.

"I look after the place. I saw you arrive just now. The camera caught you. So I came to check you weren't doing anything you shouldn't."

Janya pointed to where she had seen the woman. "Then you must have seen the woman who let me in. In a blue hood and cape. She unlocked the door."

"That couldn't happen. I keep it unlocked. That's why I put the camera there. To spy on visitors. I saw you go in alone. There was no one else. Just you. I can show you the recording if you like."

They went back out into the porch. Janya blinked in the bright sunlight.

"Lovely day," he said.

"But what about the storm? I heard thunder and wind."

"All in the mind. You wanted to believe in it all. Like the rest of them. If I were you, I'd go for a long walk in the sun. Clear your head of silly stories. You can put some coins in the box on your way out."

Janya walked from the church in a daze as a warm breeze dried her face. She was still shaking. But what if the man was right? Maybe she'd made it all up. Was it just in her mind after all? She didn't know what to think. Her head was in a spin as she climbed a stile. She sat in the shade on the disused railway line.

"All I need now is for a ghost train to run me down," she thought. But she couldn't smile. It was time for a drink. She opened her bag and looked inside. The water bottle wasn't frozen at all and her phone was working perfectly, showing her photo of the stained-glass window. She flicked through other images, then froze. The last picture showed what she didn't want to see... a woman in a blue hood and cape. She was holding a bunch of flowers in her hand. Her left hand.

Janya enlarged the image. The hand was clear... with its gold ring on the forefinger, and a ruby shining in the middle. Her fourth finger was missing completely.

There was something else in the photo. Beside the woman was a dark shape. Janya looked closely at a fuzzy image of a man in a robe at the altar. But the candles seemed to shine right through him. His arms were stretched towards the woman. But he wasn't looking at her. He was staring into the camera. A face with desperate eyes... reflecting a curling flame.

A chilling cry filled the tunnel of trees where Janya sat. It seemed to burst from her tablet...

or was it the sob of a nun carried by the wind, or just the screech of a buzzard far above the fields? She gasped as the echo circled around her before slowly drifting away on the warm summer breeze... to be drowned by the far-away shriek of startled crows.

THE SKULL

The track was overgrown with thick tangles of thistles and brambles.

"Even Indiana Jones with a flamethrower wouldn't get through all this," Ethan sighed. He scrambled up a bank to get a better look at how far the jungle of nettles stretched.

Layla wanted to get home. "Let's forget it. It's

not worth bothering."

Ethan squinted in the bright June sunlight. "I can see something. It's a roof. It must be one of the sheds. We may as well try and take a look while we're here."

Layla groaned. "It'll take all day. We only came for a quick bike ride. Why don't we come back at the weekend with shears and stuff? Dad's got loads of tools we could bring. He'll bring us in the car and we could pack a mega picnic fit for Indiana Jones."

"Hey – that's one of your best ideas yet."

Ethan and Layla had never met their old aunt – known as Great-Great-Auntie Alice. She'd died a couple of years ago when they were at primary school. Apart from sending them each a fiver every Christmas, she'd never wanted contact or visits. The old woman had locked herself away in the isolated farmhouse and kept the world far away. It was where she died at the grand age of ninety-nine. The police had to break down her front door, only to discover she'd been dead for days.

Layla and Ethan didn't go to the funeral but their mum said it was surprising how many people turned up. Some had come a long way, including a famous historian from the TV. It turned out Auntie Alice had been a well-known archaeologist and used to give lectures at museums around the world. When she retired, she retreated to her farmhouse, which she stuffed with junk. It took weeks to clear it out, before anyone could even start on the sheds and barns. But the winter set in and snowdrifts put a stop to any plans to tidy up and sell the place. Dad said it would be 'a project' for when he had time. Mum said that meant never.

SHIVERS

For most of Saturday, Ethan and Layla hacked their way up the track. Jarvis, their year-old spaniel, darted eagerly among the bracken, chasing new scents and any sticks thrown for him to retrieve. That was until a determined frenzy of swipes with a scythe finally sliced through to a dilapidated row of sheds. Most of the timber was rotten. Ivy and bindweed had long since taken hold.

"No one's been here for fifty years, I reckon," Ethan panted. "This shed's like Fort Knox. Look at those chains and locks."

They needed Dad's bolt-cutters to open the door, even though its hinges had almost rusted through. A curtain of cobwebs shimmered where bats hung from the rafters. Mice scuttled as light spilled inside. The first light for fifty years.

"Yuk. What a smell of mould. I'm not going in there!" Layla said. She stood outside while Ethan stepped into the gloom. Jarvis bounded over, only to whimper and cower before running off into the brambles.

"Help me pull the other door open, Layla. I can't see but there's something in here."

Shafts of dusty light cut through the shadows inside, where a threadbare rug covered something – just like a shroud.

"I don't like it," Layla said. "There's something scary here. I felt a weird shiver. Jarvis sensed it, too. I tell you, Ethan – I don't like it."

But Ethan was already pulling the rug to the floor in a cloud of dust. Layla sneezed and turned away. Old rat-chewed sacks slid to the ground as Ethan stood back, his mouth wide open. "Wow! Just look at that."

Layla shrugged. "Big deal."

Ethan was already wiping the bonnet. "Don't you see, Layla? It's a classic car. It could be worth a fortune." They didn't hear the sound... like something stirring.

SHIVERS

It took a week to clear the track for the pick-up truck to tow away the old car – a 1950 Morris Minor. Cousin Ben, who'd just left school to train as a motor mechanic, had agreed to restore the car as his 'project'. He couldn't wait to start work on an old Morris Minor. Even though it was in a bad way, for Ben it was like a dream come true – almost like building a car from scratch. The tyres were no good and a lot of the bodywork had rusted through. The front seats had been eaten by rats and the engine had to be completely rebuilt. But Ben knew a Morris Minor enthusiast who could get hold of parts and was keen to help. Together with a few workmates, they spent all their spare time repairing and rebuilding. Ethan and Layla came by to see what progress was being made. Jarvis refused to come anywhere near.

GHOST STORIES

Cousin Ben became obsessed with his new project. He kept on about the gearbox, cylinders and every new rivet and screw. It took over his life. Layla laughed about 'boys and their toys', while Ethan phoned him every week to ask how the car was shaping up.

"Don't worry," Ben said. "You'll soon be joining me on my first drive in it."

"Not me," Layla sneered. "That old car gives me the creeps. You'll never get me to ride in it."

Late one night while working alone, Ben removed the car's back seat. He wasn't ready for what he found hidden under it. He lifted out a small leather case full of papers. But that wasn't all. He stood back in horror. Beside it, wrapped in cloth, was a human skull.

SHIVERS

"I knew there was something weird about that car," Layla told Ben when he brought round the case. "I feel cold inside if I go anywhere near it."

"Really?" Ben said thoughtfully. "It's the opposite with me. Some nights when I'm working on it I get really hot. In fact, I often have to open the garage doors to let in fresh air. There's sometimes a really strong smell. I can't think why. Anyway, you can keep the case and do what you like with the skull. It's yours! It was probably one of Auntie Alice's museum exhibits. You might find it useful at Halloween!"

Layla began going through letters and photos in the old case. "It seems Auntie Alice drove her Morris Minor to ancient Roman sites. She wrote notes about her archaeological digs in Italy in the 1960s. Here's a photo of the car by the Colosseum. And there's Auntie Alice with her arm round a cool young guy in Venice and another at what looks like Pompeii."

Ethan looked at the photos. "Did she ever get married?"

Layla flicked through papers and letters. "I'm not sure but this note says, 'My dear Piero died while resting in my car. He was exhausted after excavating the Roman tomb and translating the obscure Latin curse he discovered. It was so sudden. I found him on the back seat with the skull in his hands. The smell was unmistakable.'"

"That's really creepy," Ethan whispered, staring at the skull wrapped in a rag beside him. "I dread to think what the smell was."

They found out when Ben phoned a week later. He was proud to report great progress with the restoration of the chassis and it wouldn't be long before the car could be driven for the first time. "The only thing is," Ben added after a long pause, "even though it's the middle of winter, I keep hearing flies buzzing inside the car. I've sprayed fly killer all over but that doesn't help. It doesn't stop the smell, either. Sometimes it's really strong, like perfume. Yesterday the whole car reeked of garlic. Weird. All that'll change once I start driving it in the fresh air with the windows open. That'll blow away the cobwebs and pongs. I'll take you both for a spin when she's ready to roll."

Layla said she didn't fancy going anywhere in the car. "I'll let you go on your own, Ethan. But hey, I've been going through more papers from that case. It looks as if Auntie Alice was writing a book about her Roman discoveries. There are lecture notes here that she's called 'Raising a Roman Stink: The Archaeology of Smell'.

Ethan couldn't help laughing. History never interested him, but he was fascinated to read his great-great-aunt's type-written introduction:

In the first and second centuries A.D., cities were very smelly places where people had to endure nasty odours. Shops and homes were mixed in together, with garlic sellers, felt makers, poultry handlers, fish sellers, perfume makers and olive oil makers. Nothing stinks more than rotting olive-oil, even 2,500 years later in excavations. With all the excrement, dead animals and sweaty gladiators in arenas, the one sound dominant in Roman times was the buzzing of millions of flies.

How did Romans try to disguise all the terrible smells on and around them? They used incense and perfume to cover up the smell of sweat — anything to hide the stench of their times.

Ethan pinched his nose to exaggerate his disgust. "That's so gross."

Layla returned to the case of papers and flicked through postcards showing ancient Roman landmarks. One showed a museum in

SHIVERS

Florence, with Auntie Alice's writing scrawled on the back: *'The curse has struck again. After the curator cleaned the skull, he placed it on display in a glass case. The next morning they found him dead in his office, with all the windows open, despite the icy wind. The skull's glass case had shattered. It's time to do something fast. I wish I'd never dug up that skull. It should be left to rest in peace. I will hide every memory of that fateful discovery. I can't bear to see my Morris Minor any more. It must all be hidden forever.'*

Layla put the card back in the case, tidied the papers inside and then shut it. "There's only one thing for it," she said. "I'll lay that skull to rest forever. I'll nail it in a wooden box and bury it at the end of the garden."

Ethan just grunted – he hadn't heard a word. His Xbox was demanding all his attention.

At the weekend, Layla dug a deep hole under a holly tree and buried the wooden box inside.

After filling the hole with soil and scattering grass seed over the top, she phoned Ben to tell him she felt sure his car would be smell-free and fine from now on. She wasn't prepared for his reply.

"The car has gone – I had to get rid of it," he began. "I'm sorry. It was making me ill. The other night I was working on it very late when I almost fainted from a sickening smell that stuck in my throat. But that's not all... the sound grew louder than ever – the angry buzzing of flies. I heard something else, though. It was the soft whisper of an Italian man, just as cold breath brushed my cheek. At first I thought my mates had played a trick or left a phone in the car. I heard the words plainly as the voice spoke in my ear. I thought he was telling me about the car, saying 'auto'. But when I asked Maria from next door to listen (she's half-Italian) she heard 'aiuto', which means 'help'. That really freaked her out

– me too. She said the voice called himself Piero. That was the final straw. I had the car taken away today... to be crushed for scrap. I'm afraid I'd had enough. That car had to be destroyed."

Layla stood at the kitchen window, thinking about the strange story. She thought about Auntie Alice and her beloved Piero, wondering how their lives could have been so different... until she glanced down the garden. The holly tree's leaves were brown and falling. They blew across the bare earth where grass seed had sprouted and died.

Nothing grew at the end of the garden. The bare patch remained where Layla had buried the box. No birds would go near. Cats kept well away. Jarvis no longer went in the back garden at all.

Ben often spoke about his project to restore the old Morris Minor and how it had all gone pear-shaped. In time, he even began to laugh about it. He was the only person ever to say the actual words: "That car was haunted, and that's all there is to it."

Just a few nights later, Jarvis was whimpering in the kitchen, trembling at the back door before throwing back his head with a chilling, ear-splitting howl.

Layla rushed outside in the darkness. Down the garden, she looked towards the skull's resting place. The holly tree was sprouting new shoots. That was a relief. Except….

Her heart missed a beat. In front of her, under the holly tree, lay the skull in the moonlight… staring up at her. The jaws were open… with jagged teeth gleaming a hideous grin.

THE LAST TRAIN

The rain was relentless. A heavy November sky descended into darkness, closing in like a tunnel of slate – as murky as the deepening black puddles reaching across the streets. Gutters gushed with the water from overflowing drains, and pavements sloshed under spewing drainpipes. By the time I'd cycled around the corner from college, my legs were soaked, my trainers were dripping and my eyes were stinging. No way was I going to ride all the way home like this.

I swerved past taxis at the railway station, jumped off my bike and squelched my way to the ticket machine. Home was just a couple of stops down the line and, as I'd often put my bike on the train in bad weather, I reckoned this was the only option on a day like this.

I checked my watch and knew I had about twenty minutes to catch the last train of the afternoon. Although it wasn't yet five o'clock, all the streetlights were splashing pools of swirling light over shiny concrete. Traffic lights reflected on wet tarmac, curdling with coloured umbrellas and oily puddles. Flashing blue lights whirled in the mix, with sirens blaring and spray spurting in all directions.

Thinking how this was the worst of all days to need an ambulance, I fed my ticket into the slot at the barrier, only to see it jam. An already stressy guard had to release the gate for me to wheel my bike through to the platform, which was heaving, probably with people like me, who had changed their plans. Soaked faces stared up at the departure board covered in DELAYED messages. Announcements that no one could hear properly blurted that all trains were running at least half an hour late.

"One drop of rain and the whole railway network grinds to a halt," an old man shouted in my ear. "I suppose it's the wrong kind of rain."

"Yeah – the wet kind," I laughed. The response was a glower as menacing as the sky. Others milling around me looked just as sullen. Nerves were frayed, patience was thin and tempers were short. The mood, like the weather, was completely dismal. It felt like one of those days when nothing goes right and all you want is to get home in the dry, while everything is determined to stop you and make life as miserable as possible.

Then came more garbled announcements:

"Apologies. Threat of floods and embankment subsidence. Slower journeys for your own safety. An incident on the line. Electrical faults and signal failure. A normal service will be resumed as soon as possible."

I wheeled my bike over the footbridge and down the steps to Platform 3, where my train was eventually meant to arrive. Others were already crammed on all the benches, and the waiting room was packed and steaming. And then the heavens opened like never before.

Doom and gloom pressed down on my dismally dreary world. After what seemed an endless, cold and miserable wait, a train eventually slid along the platform. The crowd surged forward, pushing and shoving, kicking my bike and stumbling through the doors. At last.

I propped my bike in the end carriage and squeezed my way down the aisle to look for a seat. I spotted an empty window seat, shuffled past a girl sitting next to it and slumped into it as the train lurched forward. I couldn't see out of the window as it was dribbling with lashing rain on the outside and misted up on the inside. An illegible word was scrawled across it. The letters gradually misted over completely until there was nothing left to see but the darkness beyond.

"Have you noticed how everyone looks dead gloomy?" The girl next to me was smiling, with sparkly eyes and a real chirpiness in her voice.

"Yeah, hardly surprising on a day like this," I answered glumly.

"It could be worse," she giggled. "It's a tad better than being dead, don't you reckon?"

"I'm not so sure," I smiled. "If you're dead, you don't have to worry about the rain trickling down your pants and squelching when you sit down. Sorry – too much information."

The girl snorted and flashed me the biggest grin. Her dark hair was dripping down her face, which I thought made her look really pretty.

"Life could be worse, you know!" she said brightly. "Best to make the most of it, whatever."

She wore school uniform and looked about fifteen. "As my gran always says, you're a long time dead so count your blessings while you've got them. Who cares about a bit of rain now and again? Look at my legs and shoes – plastered." Apart from smears of mud, there was what looked like a greasy tramline across her knee.

"Is that from your bike?" I asked. "I'm always getting oily marks from my bike chain."

"I haven't got a bike. Not now," she said, looking down at her phone and scrolling through her texts. "Sometimes I think I should have a cycle helmet, though," she went on. "I've got a massive bruise on my head. I'm accident prone. I really should take more care."

I could see into her bag where there were ballet shoes stuffed inside and some kind of sparkly costume.

"It looks like you dance," I said. "I've heard that dancers tend to get more injuries than people who do contact sports."

She nodded and smiled, saying nothing, then flicked through images on her phone before whispering in my ear. "Oh no, the ticket inspector's coming. I haven't got a ticket for this train. What shall I do?"

"I could cause a diversion, if you like?" I said. "How about if I turn into the Incredible Hulk and burst out of my vest, while you do the dance of the dying swan from *Swan Lake* as a distraction? It's worth a try, maybe."

She chuckled infectiously while I rummaged in my pocket. "I've got a fiver if you need it. You can pay me back another day."

"But I won't use this train again. This is the last one. I'll probably never see you again. You're so kind but I can't possibly take your money. I don't care if they fine me. It doesn't matter."

The ticket inspector stood right beside her. "Tickets, please."

She looked up at his grumpy face and beamed the biggest smile. He waited before repeating more sharply, "I said, tickets please."

"Him first," the girl smiled.

I passed him my ticket, which he clipped before grunting and turning to squint out at the lights through the window. "Next stop," he mumbled and headed to the door to open it.

"Phew, that was close," the girl said. "I'm glad you sat next to me. That could have got awkward. I hope I've helped to cheer you up. You looked down in the dumps when you sat down."

"Yeah, but you've brightened things up. Thanks. Hey, that ticket guy will be back," I warned her. "As soon as the train leaves this station, he'll come for your ticket."

"Then I'd better get off while I can," she said,

gathering her things. "I'll escape while the going's good. Thanks for the company and for making me feel better."

"You're the cheerful one," I said. "You've been a good laugh on such a miserable evening. I hope I see you again. What's your name?"

She reached across me to write on the misty window. In large letters, she scrawled 'Kelsey'.

"Nice to meet you, Kelsey," I said, as the train slowed and the platform came into view.

"Have a good life," she replied, "and always remember YOLO!"

The train stopped and she'd gone. I looked to see her get off but I was too late. Instead, I saw Sanjay from college coming down the aisle. He sat next to me with a cheery smile. "It's my lucky day – just one empty seat and it's next to you!"

"You should have seen the girl who was just sitting there. She was so cool – good looking and great fun. We were chatting all the way. *My* lucky day."

Sanjay just stared at me. "Yeah, in your dreams. I've been standing in the next carriage and I could see you all the time. This seat was empty from the minute you got on – the only spare seat on the whole train because no one dared sit next to grumpy old you. Your face looked like thunder when you got on the train." He laughed as he listened to music on his phone and hummed along with a track I didn't recognise. I pulled at one of his headphones and said sarcastically, "Well, who wrote that on the window, then? Santa Claus or maybe it's a figment of your imagination? Her name's Kelsey."

Sanjay looked at me as if I was mad and shrugged. The glass was clean and her name had gone.

"Did you see the ambulances earlier?" He was more serious now. "Apparently it was this train that caused the delays – just two stops back. Someone slipped on a wet platform and fell onto the track right in front of this train. Killed instantly. The driver had to be taken to hospital as well – because of the shock and stuff. Gruesome. Sad. YOLO."

"YOLO?"

"You only live once – so make the most of it, eh? That's my advice."

"That's weird. That's what Kelsey said."

There was something about Kelsey I couldn't get out of my mind. I was still thinking about her long after I got home and it didn't take long before I found out more. On the local TV news, I saw her face again. She flashed up on the screen – it was definitely her. Kelsey Dryden. She was in her school uniform – one of those mugshots they take at the start of the school year. She was smiling, with those same sparkly eyes. Full of life.

I froze when I heard what had happened.

GHOST STORIES

She'd slipped off a railway platform in front of a train – on her way to her ballet lesson. Kelsey died before the ambulance could arrive... just before five o'clock that afternoon.

BEHIND YOU

As teachers go, Mrs Milligan was fairly relaxed. Laid-back, even. At least, she used to be.

Before her 'anxiety attack', she thought it would be a wonderful educational experience to take her Year 6 class to what is sometimes called 'one of the most haunted cities'. Edinburgh, after all, is steeped in gruesome history and chilling tales from its ancient streets. Some of those streets are now deep underground, and it was down in these vaults where horror struck for Year 6 from Park Road Junior... and Mrs Milligan in particular.

Horror might not be quite the right word for everyone's experience. After all, one person's horror is another person's mystery. Enough to say, for Mrs Milligan, horror isn't too strong a word to describe the shivers she has experienced in her nightmares ever since...

Gathering her class together in the street, Mrs Milligan announced with a wry smile that only children who 'felt up to it' were to descend for the hour's guided tour beneath the city.

"The old town covers less than one square mile, but in the 17th century, over 60,000 people were crammed together here. Tiny rooms housed several families, and life was nasty, brutal and short. People were afraid to venture beyond the walls of the city. Crime, murder and disease took place beneath our very feet." She paused for dramatic effect. There was an audible gulp and something of a whimper from Tomas Nowak, who raised a trembling hand to ask, "Why are the old streets underground, miss?"

"Aha! A very apt question, Tomas. At some point during the 1800s the poor folks abandoned the vaults, and the whole place was sealed with rubble. No records were made, and nobody remembered them or talked about them. It wasn't until the 1980s that they were rediscovered by accident. Perhaps..." she gave an exaggerated wink, "perhaps they were sealed from the outside world with no record of their existence for a reason. Maybe to hide some terrible secret. They were then built over with the streets and buildings you see in front of you today. And who knows, we may uncover some of those secrets this very afternoon. Scary ones, at that."

Somebody squealed when a man in a long

cape appeared in front of them. "Good afternoon, everyone. I shall be your guide into the very bowels of our glorious city. Fascinating though it is to explore the streets of the past, I need to warn you that I will do all I can to keep you safe whilst underground, but alas, neither I nor the tour company can be held responsible for any supernatural injuries or shenanigans that may occur. Many ghosts are said to lurk below. People on this tour have been known to suffer heart attacks, have their skin scratched, and their hair pulled so violently that their scalps have bled. Apart from that, enjoy yourselves, don't have nightmares and follow me to the top of the steps…"

It was only then that Mrs Milligan began to have the slightest hint of doubt, but she refused to let regret show in her eyes, mainly because they were shut – as if in prayer.

"Miss, can you look after my rat in your bag,

please?" Macey Williams held up the hideous stuffed toy she'd just bought from the gift shop.

"Macey, that looks disgusting. Whatever did you buy that for?"

"To shove in my brother's bed."

"It can go out of sight in my shoulder bag next to my packet of jelly babies. Let's hope it won't nibble them. Why are they selling rats here, anyway?"

The guide butted in smugly. "All will be revealed below. Enough to say, in the summer of 1645, the worst outbreak of the plague ravaged this city. Due to overcrowding, the plague spread like wildfire, with fleas on the backs of rats transmitting the disease. So, please keep that rat well hidden, madam – or I may be forced to report you to the plague doctor. More of him later. Follow me..." He suddenly paused and with a deadpan face said, "I would ask that the teacher brings up the rear just to make sure no child is snatched into the shadows. Have you counted how many children are in this party... just in case?"

"Er yes... in this group there are twelve children and me."

"Thirteen in total. Unlucky for some..." He gave a chilling cackle, to the delight of the party – apart from Mrs Milligan. By the time she reached the bottom step and felt the cold, dark dampness seeping around her, she was longing for the tour to end.

They entered a tunnel, to more excited squeals and yelps, before descending a steep underground street, with washing hanging on lines stretched across from one upstairs window to another. The guide stopped and spoke in hushed tones.

"These streets were home to taverns, cobblers and shops, but they also had a dark side. The vaults became known as dens full of thieves, murderers, and other nasty figures, making it one of the most dangerous places in the city. Some say the ghosts of the criminals and graverobbers are still very much at home here. You are advised to cling on to your valuables... and your throats."

A faint whimper rose from the back of the party. "It's only Mrs Milligan," Macey said.

"I'll be all right in a minute," their teacher called. "It's just the change in temperature down here – I think it's got to me."

"I can't see any ghosts," Tomas piped up. "I bet it's all made up. There's no such thing."

The guide, every part the ham actor, spun around melodramatically. "Never say never, my friend. A young boy named Jack has, on many occasions, been reported grasping hold of visitors' hands or begging for food. The most famous of our ghostly apparitions is Mr Boots. If you happen to glimpse this spectral figure, he will more than likely be lingering at the back of the party..."

Mrs Milligan's whimper was louder than ever. "Your hiccups will soon pass, madam," the guide continued. "As I was saying, Mr Boots is a tall and shabby fellow with a long beard and long straggly hair. You may hear his boots echoing on the cobbles or just see him standing very still and watching you – even though some say he has no eyes. Even so, he's been known to lob stones at passers-by just to attract their attention and sometimes... ah, there he is BEHIND YOU!" He pointed with a gasp, as everyone turned to stare with excited squeals. "Oh no – sorry – a trick of the light. It's your teacher."

Everyone laughed – except Mrs Milligan. She tried to smile but couldn't. Her racing pulse was already making her feel quite sick. The next part of the talk made her feel far worse.

"We are about to enter a chamber where the stench would have been unbearable during times of plague. Pneumonic plague attacked the lungs, causing coughing that resulted in massive internal bleeding which turned the skin black, hence the name the Black Death. There was also the bubonic plague, which caused the sufferer to break out in boils filled with pus. These could swell to the size of an orange and burst, poisoning the poor sufferer's blood and often resulting in a putrid, stinking death. Are you alright, Mrs Milligan?"

"I'll be fine in a minute. I may just need a quick sit down." She slumped on a milking stool in a display in the corner.

"There's a bucket if you need it." Everyone laughed – but she feared she might.

The patter continued, much to his listeners' delight (apart from one).

"Victims of the plague were confined to rooms like this one and instructed to hang a white sheet from the window, so they would be visited by the plague doctor. George Rae was his name and he treated many people right here. He would lance the boils to let the poison run out. Then he might seal the wound with a red-hot poker, while flea-ridden rats scuttled around feeding on all the filth and festering flesh."

Gasps of delight from the audience. Groans of despair from the corner.

"Dr Rae wore a terrifying outfit to protect him from the smells that he believed to cause the plague. A long cloak kept the foul air from his skin, and he wore a beak-like mask which was filled with spices and rose petals to disguise the disgusting odours. In fact, Dr Rae's outfit probably did more good by protecting him from flea bites. You'd better all check none of you has any flea bites since coming down here – have a look at your arms and legs just in case..."

Everyone happily joined in limb examinations – apart from one. She now had her head between her knees and was close to hyperventilating. By the time more revolting stories had been vividly told and other dark nooks and crannies visited, Mrs Milligan was desperate to see daylight again. Macey sidled up to her in a particularly sinister dark passageway. "Don't worry, miss. You can hold my hand if it helps. It's brilliant down here, isn't it? It's not scary at all."

Mrs Milligan couldn't speak. It was as if her throat had frozen and her bones had turned to ice. She could just about croak, "Thank you, Macey," as the comforting hand held hers.

Tomas stood on her other side. "This is really fascinating, miss. Just say if you'd like a hand when we climb back up the slope. The others are already well ahead of us."

"Thank you, Tomas." Her words hardly came out as she reached down to grasp another comforting hand. Having two hands to grip tightly gave her the reassurance she needed to take the next steps to catch up with the party.

"This is where we all stand and look up ahead," the guide announced. "Just say 'eeeeek' as a souvenir photograph is taken, which you can purchase at the gift shop on our return to the modern world. Did anyone see, hear or feel anything that scared them to a pulp?"

"Nah," everyone chorused.

"There is still time," the guide concluded with another of his chilling cackles as he led the way back up the steps. By the time she reached the top step Mrs Milligan was beginning to feel human again. What concerned her most of all was that she couldn't explain why she'd felt so strange down there, where there was obviously nothing at all to worry about. All that hype to whip her class into a frenzy had somehow backfired and she now felt stupid in the warmer light of day. She'd turned into a nervous wreck and it didn't make sense.

"I suggest we get some refreshments and sit at

the tables in the café. I could do with a cup of coffee and some of you might like to buy souvenirs," she announced, sounding more like a normal teacher again.

"Can I buy the photograph of us all, miss?"

"It's up to you, Macey. It might be expensive. Thank you for holding my hand all the way back."

For once Macey was lost for words, frowning before whispering, "I didn't, miss."

"Well, someone else did, besides Tomas. I could have sworn it was you."

"It wasn't Tomas, either. He was at the front. You'll soon see when I get the photo..."

It didn't take long for the first anxiety attack to strike. The photograph saw to that. Instead of showing the twelve children and one teacher looking up from the ancient underground street, there were fifteen faces. For there, at the back of the party, stood Mrs Milligan looking just a little queasy. But beside her, clearly visible and holding her hands, stood a little urchin boy on one side and on the other a tall man in a long cloak, with a beak for a nose.

"That's the plague doctor," the guide exclaimed, genuinely stunned. "I've never seen him before and it isn't an actor. And as for the little boy, that's Jack. I've only seen him once before, looking for food – just look how thin he is, although he's got something green in his mouth."

Mrs Milligan couldn't drink her coffee. She needed a paracetamol. Fumbling in her shoulder bag, she pulled out an empty packet of jelly babies instead. What had been a full packet when she went down to the vaults was now empty apart from three green jelly babies – all with the heads bitten off. She gasped, clasping her hand to her mouth. No one said anything. No one knew what to say to calm down the usually laid-back Mrs Milligan. And no one dared mention what was on the back of her hand... the hand that had held the plague doctor's. It had a very fresh flea bite.

THE MIDNIGHT PASSENGER

Some dates in your life you'll always remember. They're stuck in your mind forever.

I'll never forget 1st March. Even though that particular night was years ago now, I can remember every detail. The years can never fade my memory of that chilling spring night.

The only thing I still have to prove I really

didn't imagine it all is a small pressed flower.

My first car was an old banger and things were always going wrong with it. Late on the last day of February, I was driving home from town very slowly because the rain was lashing down and my windscreen wipers were juddering and sticking. I also had a faulty back light, so I kept to the back lanes, away from any police cars. I got hopelessly lost and by midnight I had no idea where I was. The car chugged along a winding road through towering woods where branches swayed high above, twigs flying at the windscreen and rain squalling across the bonnet. I squinted out at the road ahead, where my headlights swept across the puddles. In a sudden deluge, the engine spluttered. "Don't die on me now," I cried.

Just then, as I turned the next bend and my headlights lit up a stone bridge, I saw a flash of red just ahead. It was something bright and shiny at the side of the road.

As I got closer, I saw it was a person in a red mac – a girl with soaking straggly blond hair, walking just ahead of me. I slowed down and drew alongside her. Winding down the window, I called, "Are you okay? Do you want a lift?" She didn't say anything and I couldn't see her face but the next thing I knew, she'd opened the door and was getting into the passenger seat. My inside light wasn't working so I couldn't see her clearly.

"What a foul night to be out there," I said.

She turned to face me and I caught a glimpse of a smile in the faint glow from the dashboard.

"Where do you want to get to?" I asked, as the car chugged up a steep hill in the driving rain. She just pointed at the road ahead. "Not far."

For what seemed several miles, I drove without saying much, as conversation was difficult with her one-word answers. Whenever I tried to chat, she remained silent and I didn't want to bombard her with questions, even though I was dying to know why she was out on her own in the middle of nowhere on a night like this. The swish and slap of the windscreen wipers beat time with their hypnotic rhythm, interrupted by their occasional jerky juddering. At one point I switched them on extra fast and I heard my passenger give a little giggle. I didn't want to seem nosy but eventually I couldn't stop myself saying, "I've been out with friends in town. How about you?"

There was a long pause. "Just walking," she said softly.

A fox ran across the road ahead, its eyes flashing in the headlights.

"For a second I thought it was a werewolf," I joked. "It's a bit creepy in these dark, wild woods, don't you think?"

"I like it here," she said. "It's where I feel at

home now."

"So where exactly is your home?" I asked. I wasn't expecting her answer.

"Wherever I happen to be." I wasn't expecting her question, either. "Do you like daffodils?"

I didn't know what to say. "Er... I've never eaten one!"

She didn't laugh. I felt awkward so added quickly, "Yeah, I suppose so. In their place."

"You can have one if you like. I've been picking them. Little ones grow on the banks all around here. Primroses, too. It's a good year for them. I've got plenty in my bag."

I couldn't stop myself blurting, "You've been out picking flowers on a night like this? It's just gone midnight! In fact, it's actually twenty-four minutes past twelve. It's now 1st March."

I heard a slight sigh. "If you say so. But what does time matter?"

"You obviously don't care about the weather,

either. You must be soaked through."

She laughed and rustled in her bag. I turned to look at her but the dashboard glow could only pick up her shiny wet mac. Suddenly I caught a flash of yellow.

"I'll leave you a daffodil as a souvenir. Keep it to remind you that time doesn't matter. Maybe it doesn't even exist. Clocks and calendars are just to make you believe in time."

"That's a bit heavy for this time of night," I laughed.

"What time of night? If time is an illusion, giving it a number doesn't make it any more real."

I didn't have an answer for that one. I could only grunt and comment on the rain again.

We came to a tight bend in the road. "You need to slow down here," she said.

"I've got no idea where we are. I'm completely lost. Where are we?"

"See that little light ahead? There, glinting through the trees."

"I think so."

"Can you drop me there? It's the porch light. Mum always leaves it on for me."

"Doesn't she mind you being out at all hours?"

"Hours are just measurements. You only measure if you need to control."

I didn't really understand what she meant and assumed she was just a bit weird. I began to slow down and said, "Tell me where you'd like me to stop."

"There's a little gate just ahead past this hedge."

A rickety wooden gate came into view in the beam from the headlights. I slowed right down but even before the car came to a stop, the door opened. The passenger light flickered and died but in that split second, I glimpsed the girl's hands. The knuckles were badly grazed and bruised, and what I saw of her face was smeared with mud. Without saying a word, she slammed the door shut, pulled the collar of her mac up to her head, stooped and ran off through the rain. Her shiny red mac disappeared through the gate and she'd gone. I sat with the engine running, squinting up the long path to where the light shone in the porch of a single cottage surrounded by trees. I didn't see her entering the house and wondered if she'd managed to get safely indoors. My hand brushed over the passenger seat and touched a single miniature daffodil.

I leaned over to open the passenger door to slam it again and make sure it was properly shut. The inside light flashed and I saw something glint on the floor. It was the gold clip of a small black purse. Switching off the engine, I picked up the purse, pulled up my collar against the rain and got out of the car. The rain beat down as I opened the gate, ran up the path through all the puddles and darted into the porch. The floor had red tiles, with wet footprints leading to the front door.

After knocking several times, I eventually heard a chain rattle, a bolt click, and then the door creaked open. An elderly woman peered out at me and, not wanting to scare her, I tried to explain. "Sorry to disturb you, but she left this in the car. I assume she got in alright?"

The woman looked pale, with anxious eyes, as she stared past me, straining to see my car by the gate, saying softly, "I know why you've come, dear."

"The girl in the red mac," I said. "Does she live here? Her footprints…"

I looked down but they were nowhere to be seen – there were only my footprints now.

I went on hurriedly, "She left her purse in my car." I held it out to the woman.

"Yes, that was her purse," she sighed.

"Well please pass it on to her," I gabbled. "If there's cash in it, I expect she'd like it."

The woman made no attempt to take it from me but said forlornly, "I expect she gave you a daffodil. She loved daffodils."

Now it was my turn to stare. I didn't know what to say. That's when she reached out and touched my hand, gently took the purse and held it closely to her. "It's all right, dear. You had no idea. You see, your passenger was my daughter. She was killed at the old stone bridge by a car just like yours twenty-two years ago this very night. Twelve twenty-four on the first of March. This has happened every time that the date has fallen on a Saturday."

SHIVERS

THE MUMMY'S REVENGE

arrison Garcia was the joker in the pack at Manhattan Beach Middle School. As the self-declared 'chief prankster' of sixth grade, his main aim in life was to play tricks on anyone in New York. The scarier, the better.

When it came to a project on Ancient Egyptians in class, Harrison was practically dribbling with anticipation. The more he learned about pyramids, tombs and mummies, the more his obsession grew. The day Miss Darovitz announced the forthcoming class visit to the Mummy Museum later in October, he was dangerously close to exploding with excitement. He immediately began plotting his biggest and most daring stunt ever.

Miss Darovitz, like a hen gathering her chicks around her, stood in Central Park on 31st October in bright, dappled sunlight with her class assembled, all with clipboards and worksheets labelled Mummies of Egypt and Peru.

"Now, I'm sure I don't need to remind you how to behave out here, when walking the sidewalks, crossing the streets and inside the museum."

Harrison was the only one who felt the need to answer. "Roger, Miss Darovitz."

"Now, Harrison, seeing as you have brought yourself to my attention – I can't help noticing that your backpack is considerably bigger and fuller than everyone else's. Is there a reason for that, when we're on a visit to the museum and not on a mission to Jupiter?"

"I like to be prepared for anything, Miss Darovitz. Hey, if a rocket to Jupiter shows up, I'm ready!"

He got a mixed reaction. Some laughed, others tutted at his usual irritating comments, and Miss Darovitz gave a wry smile. "Fear not, Harrison Garcia, if we happen on a space mission to anywhere, even if only to Brooklyn, I'll ensure you're on it."

That got a laugh from everyone – including Harrison. For him, as they headed down 79th Street to the American Museum of Natural History, it was like a dream come true. How could he resist the biggest Halloween fright of all time? He was prepared.

Once inside the impressively grand building,

with all eyes staring up and around at its splendour, Miss Darovitz called Harrison over for one of her 'quiet words'.

"Just a gentle warning, Harrison," she said firmly. "We are here to learn about Egyptology, not 'trickology'. Enough said? We only have an hour in this museum before it closes and I want that time well-spent. I haven't forgotten your inappropriate practical jokes last Halloween when you scared us all, not so much with your zombie costume, but because of your hysterical outbursts when setting off the fire alarm. And I haven't forgotten you 'trick or treating' outside my apartment and scaring the whole neighbourhood with your high-powered water gun firing fake blood at all the windows."

"That was so cool – but sure, Miss Darovitz, I'll be a model student today. I'm so interested in ancient mummies and their deadly curses so I can't wait to get in there for the 'Mummies

Revealed' exhibition. My favourite movies of all time are the *Night at the Museum* ones, especially all that stuff with Ancient Egyptians. I just loved it in *Secrets of the Tomb* when Larry... "

"Stop right there, Harrison. Those movies are fiction. Today we're interested in fact."

Most normal people would have left it right there but Harrison had to have the last word. "Sure thing, but what if all those ancient curses are actually real and mummies do have the power to come back to life and have their revenge?"

The withering glare from Miss Darovitz froze even Harrison. "The only thing with the power to come back to life and have its revenge, Harrison Garcia, will be my fury if you put a single foot wrong today. Got it?"

"Got it." In fact, the whole museum got it. No one messed with Miss Darovitz.

A member of staff appeared: a large man in uniform. "Hi, guys, I'm here to tell you some fascinating stuff about our mummy display and to make sure no one touches anything scary. My name's Brandon."

"Hey – you're just like him. Brundon." Harrison squealed, as Miss Darovitz closed her eyes.

"Excuse me?" Brandon frowned.

"The security guy in *Night of the Museum* was Brundon. In the movie *Battle of the Smithsonian*."

"Yeah, well I'm not Brundon, I'm Brandon. Now, just to tell you some facts. You'll see a beautifully preserved Egyptian mummy with a gilded headdress and painted facial features She has never been unwrapped since she was carefully preserved thousands of years ago."

Harrison couldn't resist. "Well I've got some scissors in my backpack. Why not give it a go? By the way, is it true that anyone who glimpses her unwrapped form will be cursed to die a horrific death?"

"It can certainly be arranged," Brandon sighed

impatiently and continued his prepared speech, which he was determined not even Harrison would manage to hijack. "Mummification involved drying out a dead body to preserve it for the next life. Egyptians believed that the liver, lungs, stomach and intestines needed to be preserved because the person would need all these body parts in the afterlife. The organs were placed in a small stone or wood chest divided into four compartments or into canopic jars like the ones you will see. The jackal-headed jar, for instance, would have held a person's stomach that had been carefully dried and wrapped in linen. Any questions so far?"

Harrison's hand shot up. "Yeah. What would happen if I touched one of the mummies, Brundon?"

"Brandon. Don't even think about it, kid. I'm a black belt and I weigh 250 pounds. Any other questions?"

GHOST STORIES

Harrison wasn't giving up. "Yeah – have you ever stayed in the museum all night and have you seen any mummy ghosts in here?"

Brandon kept a deadpan face while turning to the rest of the group and winking, which only they could see. "Only at Halloween. One of our mummies has been known to come to life and follow home any annoying sixth-grader." Miss Darovitz and the class roared with laughter. Harrison was open-mouthed, already lost in his own imagination.

"Now follow me and I will reveal to you the secrets of the past." Brandon led the way into an atmospheric exhibition room, dimly lit, cool and eerily quiet. Once inside, his voice became a hypnotic whisper. "We now know exactly what lies inside those coffins and bandages. CT scans of the Field Museum's mummies in Chicago have shown us bones, muscles, and even the hair of the persons inside their wrappings and coffins.

And did you know, we also have cat mummies in here, so make sure one doesn't sneak up and scratch you, Harrison."

"How do you know my name?"

"My mummy told me."

The tour was fascinating and the exhibits mesmerizing. For most of the class, being able to connect with people from thousands of years ago was amazing enough, but Harrison wanted more. His obsession with ghosts, Halloween and nights in museums was taking over. "Excuse me, Miss Darovitz, is it okay for me to visit the restroom?"

He didn't notice the look in her eyes. "If you must, Harrison. Just follow those signs and be back here promptly as we shall be leaving in five minutes."

"Sure – don't go without me!" he called as he ran from the room.

As soon as Harrison locked himself in a

cubicle, he opened his backpack to unravel the packed rolls of bandages, tape and make-up. He began by winding a toilet roll around his ankle, spiralling it upwards around his knee and leg. Chuckling to himself as he transformed into the scariest mummy imaginable, he concentrated on taping down and pinning loose ends, to ensure nothing would unravel during his grand entrance, when all heads were bound to turn. Maybe some visitors would faint and others would run screaming from the building. It would go down as the most impressive 'trick or treat' on record.

The transformation from sixth-grader to grotesque member of the walking dead took longer than Harrison intended. It was trickier than expected binding himself up in such a cramped space without a mirror and no one to help with safety pins. Eventually, when emerging from his cubicle, he caught sight of himself in the mirror and squealed with excitement. Perfect. He practised a suitable plod – more like a lurch with a stagger and an occasional drag of his foot. After all, he assumed that after being dead for three thousand years, he'd be unlikely to walk at his best.

At last, the walking mummy hobbled through the door and towards the exhibition hall. Unfortunately, he couldn't see where he was going, partly because a flap of bandage had slipped over his eyes, and partly because it was now very dark. Only when he realised all the lights were off and that the place was totally silent, did he suspect he'd taken far longer than planned. So long, in fact, that everyone had gone and the museum was closed for the night.

Entering the scarily dark and deserted Egypt Room, with its deep shadows and sphynx silhouettes towering against a far street-lit window, Harrison gulped at the terrifying thought; he was alone for a night at the museum.

He walked the length of the huge room containing shadowy hieroglyphs, in the vain hope that the janitor might still be mopping the floor or rattling a key. Harrison gingerly approached the decorated coffin bathed in eerie moonlight from a skylight. He heard a creek, then a deep groan... followed by a menacing sigh from inside the coffin. He froze, unable to move, as a death mask right in front of his nose gave a single sinister wink. As if that wasn't enough to send him scuttling into the arms of a pharaoh's statue, he was sure he glimpsed a bandaged hand clawing at a sarcophagus.

When a mummified gazelle and canopic jars of a baboon, hawk and jackal slowly rotated in a spooky purple glow, Harrison ran from the room, screaming. He hurtled down the corridor back to the rest room, threw himself at his backpack and fumbled for his cell phone. Within seconds, he was shrieking, "Mom, you gotta get me outta here!"

"What's up, honey?" asked his mother, sounding unusually calm.

"I'm stuck in the museum. It's Halloween and I'm petrified."

"Well that sounds like just the sort of thing you'd like, Harrison."

"Mom, you've gotta listen to me!"

"This could just be another of your tricks. Could this be one of your mischievous pranks or is it a case of the boy who cried wolf? There again, it could be more of a case of the boy who wants his mummy."

"Mom – HELP!"

"Just calm down, honey. Take yourself from the rest room into the Egypt Room and someone will meet you there."

"But what if it's a mummy on the prowl? Hey... how do you know I'm in the restroom?"

"See you in a minute, honey."

GHOST STORIES

As soon as Harrison crept from his hiding place, he could see the blaze of lights in the Egypt Room and could hear the cheers. As he shuffled in to the applause and yelps of his class, his bandages unravelling with every step, he looked up at his mother grinning at him.

"We thought you'd appreciate a 'trick or treat' joke to remember, Harrison. But keep your costume on as we've got a mummy-themed party back home for your friends right now."

For once he was speechless, as Miss Darovitz greeted him with, "We all knew you were planning something scary, Harrison – so we just thought we'd play you at your own game. The museum staff were more than happy to join in. Maybe you'll think twice next time you plan to scare us all."

Brandon shook him by the hand. "No hard feelings, buster? Come and look at how we fixed all those special effects. Just a few lighting techniques, sound effects operated remotely, and various objects placed on rotating mats triggered by sensors when you got close. Clever, huh?"

By now Harrison was grinning. "Hey, that's so awesome. Fair play, everyone, you really got me going this time. Just one thing... How did you get the death mask to wink so creepily?"

Astonishment. Worried looks. After a very long and awkward pause, Brandon tried to speak. "We didn't," he stuttered, his face draining of all its colour. "That was nothing to do with us."

"But I saw it with my own eyes!" Harrison exclaimed.

"In that case, I'm afraid you need to know," Brandon sighed, with a look of genuine horror. "An ancient legend says that anyone seeing the eyes move on that death mask will be visited by the mummy's ghost, seeking revenge at the next full moon."

An icy shiver passed through the Egypt Room and everyone was stunned into deathly silence.

SOMETHING IN THE CELLAR

Female college student offers babysitting service. Reasonable rates. Good with children. Ages 3-10 preferred. References available.

Within hours of posting her card in a window of the grocery store, Madison received a call.

SHIVERS

"Can you manage Saturday evening? I can collect you at 6 o'clock and return you home shortly after midnight. We're happy to pay double your normal rate. Our children are Bobbie, aged six, and Tamsin, aged four. They're well-behaved and sleep like little angels. They'll be no trouble at all. We live in West Moorside."

Madison couldn't believe her luck. West Moorside was the exclusive area with enormous mansions and beautiful gardens. It sounded so ideal that she accepted immediately and happily gave her details. When a top-of-the-range Maserati Quattroporte arrived to collect her on Saturday evening, she was thrilled she'd agreed to the job. The luxurious car was driven by the children's mother who announced, as they drove up a tree-lined drive to a formidable mansion, "My husband and I will only be across town so just give us a call if there's a problem. I've left our number by the phone in the hall. You can come and meet the children in their basement playroom before they go up to bed in about an hour."

As soon as Madison stepped inside the vast hallway, with its ornate central staircase, she was staggered to see a wealth of antique furniture, clocks and paintings. A man in a smart suit appeared and read her mind. "It's my business. I work in the antique trade. Hi, I'm Denzel. Come with me downstairs and meet the kids."

He led the way down a spiral staircase and into a large, beautifully furnished room where two children, already dressed for bed, were absorbed in a movie on an enormous flat-screen TV. After their introductions, Denzel told her, "Once the kids are in bed, they'll soon go to sleep. You can read them a story if you like. Nothing about circuses as they've got a thing about clowns. Apparently the previous owners ran a circus and kept stuff for it down here in what was then a filthy old cellar, so they've got some funny ideas. Now it's our playroom basement and it's where you can watch TV and relax when they're asleep. There's a fridge, kettle, drinks and sandwiches and plenty of DVDs so just help yourself. But please stay in this room – the rest of the house is strictly off-limits."

Both parents kissed the children goodnight, told Madison they'd be back just after midnight and then left. It was already dark outside and before long Tamsin was yawning and struggling to keep awake, so it was definitely bedtime. "I'll take you up first," Madison said.

"I'm coming up, too," Bobbie insisted. "I'm not staying in this room on my own."

"Why's that?" she asked.

"I don't like the clown who once lived here."

"Clowns are so funny, aren't they, Bobbie?" Madison wasn't sure what else to say.

"Not Gribaldi."

"Well, never mind about that now, let's go upstairs, shall we?" She held their hands and they led her up two flights of stairs onto a wide landing full of paintings and ornaments. As they walked on a thick white carpet past a painting of a jolly-looking bearded man in frills and a big hat, Bobbie covered his eyes. "Daddy calls him the Laughing Cavalier and I don't like him. His eyes are always staring at me."

"I expect he's just making sure you're all right," she said. "I think he looks nice and friendly."

"Not in the middle of the night when he laughs," Tamsin said, very matter-of-fact.

Madison smiled. She liked children with so much imagination and sparkle, remembering how she had also been scared of clowns and fancy-dressed characters when she was little. After reassuring the children and reading them both a story until their eyelids grew heavy, she tucked them up, turned the lights down low and tiptoed onto the landing. It was all so easy. She waited at their doors until she was convinced they were both asleep, then made her way back along the landing, smiling at the Laughing Cavalier on the way. She could see why Bobbie didn't like him, as she also felt the eyes watching her all the way to the stairs. Once back down in the basement, she sat on the sofa, put her feet up and watched the big 3D screen with its amazing sound system. She cast her eyes around the room, with its stylish subdued lighting, at all the expensive furnishings and fittings. In one corner, a velvet drape covered something tall – maybe a large toy of some sort. As she tried to work out what it might be from its strange shape, she was sure she saw it move slightly. There again, it could just have been the flickering light from the TV.

With curiosity getting the better of her, Madison got up and went across the room towards the cloaked shape, staring at the rounded top and wondering if it was some kind of floor lamp topped with a glass globe. She touched the velvet and pulled it slightly so it began to slide off. She stood back and gasped as the cover fell to the floor and a life-sized statue of a clown stared back at her, with an enormous painted grin. It looked hideous and had a sign round its neck: 'The Great Gribaldi'. She threw the cover back over it and wondered why anyone would want to own a thing like that. Now she knew why Bobbie had a thing about clowns. If that statue repulsed her, no wonder it freaked out the children.

Wondering how common the fear of clowns might be, Madison sat back on the sofa with her smartphone and did a search. The word 'coulrophobia' reassured her that many others would also be troubled by that grotesque statue behind her. She read an explanation: 'Clowns are meant to be characters of innocent fun – brightly coloured jesters to entertain our children by slipping on banana skins and performing other displays of slapstick comedy. But the fun and exaggerated mask of thick make-up are just a breath away from terror'.

When she searched for Gribaldi, she shivered at what she saw. 'The Great Gribaldi was a popular circus clown all around the world in the mid-20th century. His career came to a tragic end after an act went wrong – he was fired from a cannon and broke his neck. He died a few weeks later at his home in West Moorside.'

However much she tried to concentrate on a game show on the screen in front of her, Madison grew increasingly concerned about the presence behind her. She kept turning around to look at the cloaked shape in the corner. She knew she was getting over-anxious when she looked behind yet again and felt sure it had moved away from the corner slightly. Despite the cover hiding its horrible face, she couldn't shake off the feeling that the clown was able to see her, and was watching her every move. She knew it was ridiculous, but to put her mind at rest, she went into the adjoining bathroom, grabbed a large, thick towel and gingerly approached the statue. Not wishing to get too close, she stood on a footstool, leaned forward with outstretched arms and tied a blindfold around the head. It was as she pulled it as tightly as she could that she heard a crack and felt the head tilt to one side. She screamed, toppled off the stool and scrambled to the other side of the room, staring with horror as the clown with the broken neck gave a blood-curdling groan.

In a fit of mad panic, Madison ran from the room, up the spiral stairs, into the hallway and snatched at an ornate phone on a polished mahogany table. Tapping in the number on the phone pad, she trembled as it bleeped for what seemed forever, before Denzel finally answered.

"Please, Denzel... I know you said I mustn't go

in any other rooms but can I go somewhere else in the house to get away from the basement? I'm really freaked out by your statue of the clown."

After the briefest of pauses, he shouted back at her, "You must get out of the house NOW. We don't have a clown statue. The children have been telling us they've been seeing a clown in their rooms at night, and we just thought they were having nightmares. Take the children and get out quick!"

Madison hung up and ran back downstairs to fetch her bag and phone... but didn't get that far. At the door to the basement, she shrieked when she saw the statue had gone. The velvet drape and towel were lying on the floor. Without looking back, she clambered up the stairs to the hallway, where she froze at the sound of a child crying, just as a spine-chilling chuckle descended from somewhere just above...

GHOST STORIES

SHIVERS

GHOSTLY FACTS

Did you know....

1. *The Rabbit's Foot* is based on a story written by an English writer of novels and short stories: W W Jacobs (1863–1943). *The Monkey's Paw* was published in 1902 and has inspired many stories, films and plays ever since.

2. From the Bible to *Macbeth*, to the latest horror movies, ghosts have been fascinating subjects ever since people first started telling stories. They're also big business for Halloween merchandise, especially in the US. About 180 million Americans celebrate Halloween. Total spending in 2017 was over US $9 billion, with the average consumer spending US $86 on decorations, candy, costumes and more.

GHOST STORIES

3. Many surveys have shown that around 45% of people believe in ghosts, spirits and paranormal activity. A YouGov poll in 2014 reported that 39% of the people surveyed in the UK believed that a house can be haunted by some kind of supernatural being, and almost as many (34%) thought that ghosts actually exist.

4. Some people think a sure sign of a ghost's presence is when a candle flame burns blue or suddenly goes out with no apparent draught or breeze. Scientists might well explain such things differently!

5 The White House is reported to be haunted by a number of ghosts, including that of Abigail Adams, who has reportedly been seen hurrying towards the East Room, where she used to hang her laundry.

6. For many years, presidents, first ladies, guests and members of the White House staff have claimed to have seen former president Abraham Lincoln (1809–1865) or felt his presence. Sightings of Lincoln's ghost were reported during the presidency of Franklin D. Roosevelt, as the country struggled through the 1930s economic Depression, followed by World War II. The Netherlands' Queen Wilhelmina was a guest at the White House during that period, and was apparently woken one night by a knock on her bedroom door. On opening the door, she saw the figure of Lincoln in a top hat standing in the hallway. The queen fainted – obviously!

7. The fear of ghosts is called 'phasmophobia'. The word comes from the Greek word 'phasmos', which means 'supernatural being/phantom' and 'phóbos', which means

'deep dread or fear'. Another word for it is 'spectrophobia', which originates from 'spectres' or 'reflection'.

8. The fear of clowns (as in 'Something in the Cellar') is coulrophobia. This may come from the Greek word 'kolon' meaning stilt or stilt-walkers – stilts are often used by clowns. Coulrophobia is fairly common, particularly among children.

9. According to the Guinness Book of World Records, the largest gathering of people dressed as ghosts is 560 people and was achieved by Mercy School Mounthawk in Tralee, Ireland, on 24 March 2017.

10. Also in the Guinness Book of World Records is the loudest scream ever recorded. Classroom assistant Jill Drake (UK) had

a scream that reached 129 decibels when
measured at the Halloween festivities held
in the Millennium Dome, London, UK in
October 2000. (An air raid siren is 135 decibels
and a jet engine at take-off is 140!)

11. The first reporded sighting of a poltergeist
– a ghost that makes noises and throws objects
– is in 856 AD in a farmhouse in Germany. It
is said that a family living there was terrorised
by the entity, which threw stones at them and
started fires.

12. Some famous people who claim to have
seen ghosts include the poet Lord Byron, rock-
star Mick Jagger of The Rolling Stones, Queen
Elizabeth II and former British prime minister
Winston Churchill.

13. Ghosts of lots of famous people have supposedly been sighted. Celebrity ghosts include Anne Boleyn, Guy Fawkes, Oliver Cromwell and John Lennon.

14. The Ancient Romans believed that if you scratched a curse on a shard of pottery and left it in a grave, the restless spirit within would exact revenge on someone on your behalf.

15. Ghosts were very fashionable in the Victorian era. High-society ladies would host séances at their homes, where prominent guests would sit in a circle and try to contact the spirit world in order to receive messages from the dead.

16. In the late 19th century, ghost clubs were formed at Oxford and Cambridge universities to hunt for evidence of the supernatural. The

most important and prestigious organisation, the Society for Psychical Research, was founded in 1882. It was led by an investigator called Eleanor Sidgwick.

17. One rational explanation suggested for why people think they've seen or felt a ghostly presence is that electromagnetic fields in some places might have interfered with their brain activity. Another is that inaudible vibrations and low-frequency noises might confuse people and make them uneasy so they see things that are not really there. British engineer Vic Tandy wrote a scientific paper in 1998 about how he felt uncomfortable working in one particular lab and then discovered that this was due to the vibrations caused by a fan circulating air in the room. He proposed that such unnoticed vibrations could be the ordinary cause of many supernatural experiences.

GLOSSARY

archaeologist someone who digs up the remains of ancient buildings and objects in order to learn about the past.

folklore the beliefs and stories of a particular community that have been passed down from generation to generation via word of mouth.

subsidence when an area of land slowly begins to sink or cave in.

supernatural something that is seemingly outside of the natural laws of the universe and the scientific understanding of the world.

The Laughing Cavalier a famous portrait painting by the Dutch painter Frans Hals, created in 1624 AD.